Date Due

Text copyright © 1999 by Russell Hoban
Illustrations copyright © 1999 by Quentin Blake
First American edition 2000 published by Orchard Books

First published in Great Britain in 1999 by Faber and Faber Limited

Russell Hoban and Quentin Blake assert the right to be named as the
author and the illustrator of this work.

Orchard Books, A Grolier Company
95 Madison Avenue, New York, NY 10016

Manufactured in Singapore
The text of this book is set in 15 point Sabon.
The illustrations are pen and ink with watercolor.
10 9 8 7 6 5 4 3 2 1

Library of Congress Cataloging-in-Publication Data
Hoban, Russell.
Trouble on Thunder Mountain / by Russell Hoban ; pictures by
Quentin Blake. p. cm.
Summary: When Megafright International flattens their beautiful
mountain to put up a hi-tech plastic theme park, the O'Saurus family
uses faith and lots of Monsta-Gloo to put things right.
ISBN 0-531-30206-7 (trade : alk. paper)
[1. Dinosaurs—Fiction. 2. Mountains—Fiction.]
I. Blake, Quentin, ill. II. Title.
PZ7.H637Tt 1999 [Fic]—dc21 99-18155

For Paulchen—R.H.

Thunder
Mountain

The Family O'Saurus

to Endsville

Mom O'Saurus and Dad O'Saurus and
their son, Jim, had lived on Thunder Mountain
for ages and ages, and they were very happy
there. They grew parsnips and leeks and onions
and potatoes in their vegetable patch, and they
grew rocks in their rock garden.

They had a TV and a VCR, and they watched movies like *Rocky Dinosaur—Secret Agent, Rocky Dinosaur on the Orient Express,* and *Rocky Dinosaur's Return Trip.* They also enjoyed *The Extinct Road Show* and *Mesozoic Challenge.*

One day the postman brought them a letter:

Dear Family O'Saurus,

I am delighted to tell you that Thunder Mountain has been bought by Megafright International. We are going to make it flat and build a hi-tech plastic-mountain theme park on the flat place. This will be called Megafright Mountain, and it will have robot monsters and a Tunnel of Terror and other scary rides. We are ready to start work now, so you have twenty-four hours (beginning yesterday) to get out.

Megafrightfully yours,

J. M. Flatbrain, President

"A hi-tech plastic mountain," said Dad.

"It takes a man named Flatbrain to think of something like that," said Jim.

"Listen!" said Mom. "I hear heavy machinery coming up the road. I am worried about our vegetable patch."

"Maybe we could stomp on him and his machines and show him what flatness is all about," said Jim.

"Jim," said Dad, "any fool can resort to violence, but that is not our way."

"What are we going to do then?" said Jim.

"I do not know," said Dad, "but I will think of something."

"Better do it soon," said Mom. "There go the parsnips."

"Good morning," said Mr. Flatbrain. "Now it is time for you to leave, because we are going to start blasting."

"We do not want to leave," said Dad. "This is *our* mountain, and we want to stay here."

"This is not your mountain anymore," said Mr. Flatbrain. "Now it belongs to Megafright International."

"Thunder Mountain is so beautiful," said Mom. "How can you want to flatten it?"

"Thunder Mountain is just a lot of dirt and rocks, with creepy-crawlies under the rocks and animals running around loose all over the place," said Mr. Flatbrain. "Megafright Mountain will be clean and tidy, with entertainment for the whole family and no ants when they picnic." He gave Dad a piece of paper. "There is a place for you down the road. Good-bye and good luck."

The O'Sauruses loaded up their belongings onto their old pickup truck. They loaded their TV and VCR and their beds and sofas and tables and chairs. They loaded their curtains and carpets and pictures and bric-a-brac. They loaded their dishes and their pots and pans, their croquet set and camping gear. They loaded their toolboxes and their buckets and wheelbarrows and shovels and pickaxes. They took a bag of seed potatoes with them too.

"Have you packed the Monsta-Gloo?" said Mom to Dad.

"Yes," said Dad. "Everything is packed."

Off they went down the road. All the animals and birds from Thunder Mountain followed them. After a while they found a garbage dump full of broken bottles, rusty bedsprings, broken bathtubs, and car seats with the stuffing coming out. Mom and Dad and Jim looked at their piece of paper. It said:

```
Dear Family O'Soupus,
    This garbage dump has been reserved
for you. We hope you will be pleased
with this impravement.
    Betterly yours,
    A. Worser
```

"Worser could do better with his spelling," said Jim.

"That is the least of our worries," said Dad.

"This is a very ugly place," said Mom.

"It is very flat as well," said Jim.

"We will never sing here," said the birds.

"This ground smells bad," said the moles. "We do not want to dig here."

"This is not a very nice place, but we are going to have to make the best of it," said Mom.

Just then they heard a big bang, and they saw the top of Thunder Mountain go up into the air.

"You said you would think of something," Jim said to Dad.

"I am thinking," said Dad, "but nothing has come to me."

"I am thinking too," said Mom, "and I have an idea. But we will need a little faith and a lot of Monsta-Gloo for it to work."

"We have plenty of both," said Dad.

"Tell us what to do," said Jim.

"First we need to see what they are doing with the pieces of our mountain," said Mom.

After the robot monsters loaded the pieces onto their trucks and drove away, the O'Sauruses and their friends followed them. They were careful to keep out of sight.

When the trucks came to a beautiful valley, Mr. Flatbrain said to his robot-monster foreman, "Dump everything here, and we will fill in this valley and make it flat."

"Okay, boss," said the robot-monster foreman, and all the trucks dumped their loads in the valley.

When the Megafright trucks drove off, Mom said to everyone, "Do you know what I have in mind?"

"Yes," they said. They loaded all the pieces of the top of Thunder Mountain into the pickup truck. When they got back, they stuck them together with Monsta-Gloo.

When Mr. Flatbrain and his crew came back to dump again, they could not find what they had dumped before. "Amazing," said Mr. Flatbrain. "Everything seems to have sunk right into the ground."

As soon as the Megafright trucks went back to the mountain, the O'Sauruses and their friends came with the pickup truck and loaded up again. They had to build quite a large crane to lift up the top of the mountain so that they could slide the next part under it. They stuck it together with Monsta-Gloo.

"This is hard work," said Jim.

"Sometimes there is no easy way," said Dad, "but little by little we are getting it together."

"I think we should put up a curtain," said Mom, "for privacy."

"Good idea," said Dad and Jim. Everybody got busy with needle and thread, and they made a great big curtain. Then they made a frame to hang it on.

The Megafright trucks made many more trips, and so did the O'Sauruses. Mr. Flatbrain did not notice the curtain until his plastic mountain was almost finished. "What is happening behind that curtain?" he said to his robot-monster foreman. "What are those noises I hear?"

"Bzzz, klonk," said the robot-monster foreman. "Maybe big party?"

"Maybe you should lift a corner of the curtain and have a look," said Mr. Flatbrain.

"Zing, zang, pfeh, pfft," said the robot-monster foreman.

"What are you trying to say?" said Mr. Flatbrain.

"Got problem," said the robot-monster foreman. "No software for lift curtain."

Mr. Flatbrain kicked the robot-monster foreman. "Try," he said.

"Pfeh," said the robot-monster foreman. It lifted one corner of the curtain and went inside. Dad was waiting for it with a screwdriver and a wrench.

"What can you see?" said Mr. Flatbrain.

"Dark, boss. Bzzz, burp. Very dark," said Dad in a robot-monster voice as he dressed up in the robot-monster parts as well as he could.

"Look again," said Mr. Flatbrain.

"Big screen, boss," said Dad. "Pictures moving. Heavy thriller." He made noises like the movie *Rocky Dinosaur—Secret Agent.*

"That sounds like *Rocky Dinosaur—Secret Agent,*" said Mr. Flatbrain. "Are there a lot of people watching it?"

"Hundreds," said Dad.

"Good," said Mr. Flatbrain. "That means there will be good crowds on Megafright Mountain. Now you should get back to work."

"Okay, boss," said Dad. He came out from behind the curtain in his robot-monster foreman disguise.

"You look bigger than you did before," said Mr. Flatbrain.

"Feel great," said Dad.

"I am going back to the office now," said Mr. Flatbrain. "Tomorrow is opening day, and I want Megafright Mountain all finished and ready."

"Right!" said Dad. "Tomorrow all finish."

Behind the curtain, the O'Sauruses and their
friends had Thunder Mountain all put together.
As soon as Mr. Flatbrain left, they put wheels
under it and moved it next to Megafright
Mountain. Among the O'Sauruses' friends were
four hundred mole technicians and two or three
thousand ants.

"There are the robots," said Dad to the ants. "You know what to do."

"Everything is go," said the ants. They crawled into the robots and changed their circuits.

"Bzzz, klonk, bzzt," said Dad. "This mountain— take apart."

"No problem," said Robot Monster Number One. The robot monsters took Megafright Mountain apart.

Then the O'Sauruses and their friends moved the real mountain back to where it used to be.

"Bzzt, burp," said Dad to the robot monsters. "Make tunnel."

The robot monsters made a tunnel in the real mountain.

"Zing, zang," said Dad. "Put in tracks for little train."

The robot monsters put in tracks all the way to Endsville many, many miles away.

"Put in little train," said Dad.

The robot monsters loaded all the pieces of Megafright Mountain and the Tunnel of Terror onto the little train. Then they sent the train to Endsville.

The O'Sauruses and their friends got ready
for opening day. They put up signs:

SINGALONG WITH BIRDS!

They also put up another sign:

TUNNEL TO MEGAFRIGHT MOUNTAIN THIS WAY →

Mr. Flatbrain arrived early on opening day. "What is all this?" he roared. "It is all dirt and rocks and creepy-crawlies again. What happened to Megafright Mountain?"

"Bzzz, klonk," said Dad. "Please, this way." He led Mr. Flatbrain to the tunnel entrance. He put him on the little train and sent him off to Endsville.

Then the O'Saruses set up a stand on their mountain, and they put up a sign:

Many people bought packed lunches and picnicked on the mountain. Some of them had never seen a mountain before. They met the animals.

They sang along with the birds. They interacted with the ants. Everyone had a good time.

Others followed the signs to the tunnel, got on the little train, and ended up in Endsville. There they saw Mr. Flatbrain trying to put the plastic mountain and the Tunnel of Terror back together again.

Everyone helped, but it took a year and a half.

When it was finished, everyone said, "It looks like a plastic mountain."

After the Tunnel of Terror was in place, everyone tried it out. Then some began to mutter. Others began to shout. "Megafright Mountain is not as good as a real mountain, and the Tunnel of Terror is boring," they shouted.

Mr. Flatbrain became megafrightened, and he ran away to a town where nobody knew him.

He became a gardener and made rock
gardens in the shape of little mountains.
Sometimes he made tunnels in them.